Mad About

Spiders,

bugs,

and other

insects

make
believe
ideas

Spiders

With their hairy, scary legs, **spiders** are some of the most feared creatures around! Unlike other bugs, spiders can spin silk **webs** to catch their food.

feeler

Black widow spider

Jumping spider

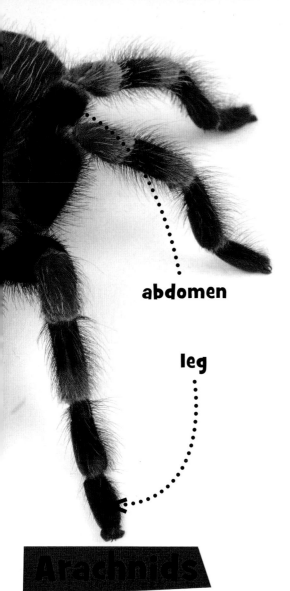

abdomen

leg

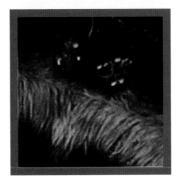

eyes

web

Arachnids

Spiders are not insects.
They are **arachnids**.
They have eight legs
and two or four feelers.

Mad about spiders

A spider's silk is very thin. But for its size it is stronger than steel.

Most spiders have eight eyes!

The largest spider is a type of Huntsman spider. It would be as big as this page!

Jumping spiders can live in very high places. They have even been found on Mount Everest.

Scorpions

Scorpions are **arachnids** armed for attack and defense! They have powerful pincers and a **sting** at the end of their tail. They use their sting to **stun** their victims.

mouth

Emperor scorpion

pincer

Mad about scorpions

Scorpions are prehistoric creatures. Some lived as long as 400 million years ago!

Scorpions can have up to twelve eyes but they can't see very well. They usually hunt by touch.

Some scorpions can live for a year without food or water!

Female scorpions give birth to live babies, which they carry around on their backs.

pincer

sting

Scary stingers

A scorpion's **sting** can be deadly. However, scorpions mainly use their sting in **self-defense**.

Desert hairy scorpion

Beetles

head

thorax

Beetles are **insects**. This means that they have **six legs** and their body is divided into **three sections**—the head, thorax, and abdomen.

Rainbow Christmas beetle

Scarab beetle

Taurus beetle

Most **beetles** can fly. They open their front wings and beat their large, papery back wings.

Ladybug

Rhinoceros beetle

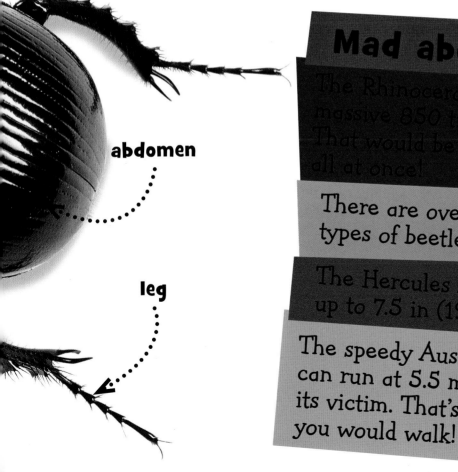

abdomen

leg

Mad about beetles

The Rhinoceros beetle can lift a massive 850 times its own weight. That would be like lifting 10 cars all at once!

There are over 350,000 known types of beetle!

The Hercules beetle can grow up to 7.5 in (19 cm) long. Eek!

The speedy Australian tiger beetle can run at 5.5 mph (9 kph) to catch its victim. That's twice as fast as you would walk!

Ants

Ants live in large groups called **colonies**.
A colony can contain less than 100 ants,
or more than a million! Each ant is
given a specific **role** in order to
look after the colony.

thorax

head

abdomen

flying ant

ant hill

Mad about ants

Female worker ants take care of the colony, while the queen ant rules the roost!

Driver ants live in Africa in huge colonies. Together they can kill animals as large as cows!

Queen ants can live to be over ten years old.

Crafty, slave-making ants steal unborn ants from other colonies and bring them up as their slaves!

feeler

Ant smells

Ants can give out unique **smells** to warn other ants of dangers or obstacles up ahead.

leg

Bugs!

Use your stickers to create a crazy bug scene.

Caterpillars

A **caterpillar** hatches from an egg and keeps eating until it is big enough to make a safe shell, or **chrysalis.** When it is ready, the caterpillar comes out of the shell as a **butterfly** or a **moth**.

Swallowtail caterpillar

Gypsy moth caterpillar

Io moth caterpillar

front leg

Mad about caterpillars

Many caterpillars have similar patterns and colors to the food they eat. Imagine looking like your favorite dinner!

Caterpillars usually have three pairs of legs in the front and up to five pairs of false legs, or suckers, in the back.

Caterpillars have 4,000 muscles in their body—we have less than 700 muscles!

caterpillar feeding

chrysalis

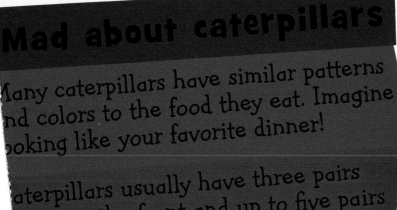

false leg

Butterflies

Butterflies start their life as **caterpillars**. They have four **wings** that work together like a single pair of wings.

antenna

leg

front wing

back wing

abdomen

Swallowtail butterfly

proboscis

eye

Mad about butterflies

The largest butterfly is the Queen
Alexandra Birdwing. It has a wingspan
of over 11 in (28 cm). Find a ruler and
see how wide that is!

Butterflies feed on the sticky, sweet nectar
found in flowers. They drink it through
a built-in straw called a proboscis!

Butterflies are among the most colorful
insects, but they can only see in red,
yellow, and green.

Frequent flyers

Monarch butterfly

Monarch butterflies travel an
amazing 3,000 miles (4,800 km)
every year to avoid cold winters.

Bees

Honeybees live together in groups or **colonies**. Within the group, each bee has its own job: the **queen bee** lays eggs, **drone bees** mate with the queen, and **worker bees** collect nectar and pollen from flowers to make the **honeycomb**.

wing

collecting nectar

honeycomb

Mad about bees

The smallest bee is no bigger than your little fingernail!

Bees are the most useful insects in the world. They carry pollen from flower to flower. This helps to make new seeds, which eventually grow into beautiful new plants.

Some people are so mad about bees, they wear them! In a record-breaking attempt, one man covered himself with over 300,000 bees.

A queen bee can lay up to 2,000 eggs a day!

pollen basket

Nectar and pollen

As a **bee** hunts for nectar, pollen sticks to its hairy coat. The bee combs it into the **pollen baskets** on its back legs and uses it to feed the young grubs in the hive.

Stick insects

Stick insects have one of the most
effective ways of hiding from attackers.
By looking like a stick or a leaf,
they can **blend** into their
surroundings with ease.

eye

foot

tail

leg

Giant spiny stick insect

Mad about stick insects

Stick insects are the longest known insects. With their legs stretched out, they can be 22 in (55 cm) long. That's as long as three new pencils put together!

Stick insects usually move around at night and stay very still during the day.

Some stick insects lay more than 2,000 eggs!

To avoid being eaten, stick insects will lose a leg and even fake death!

Molting

As they grow, **stick insects** shed their skin several times. Underneath is a new, bigger skin. This is called **molting**.

Guess who?

Look at the pictures, read the clues, and guess what each bug is.

1 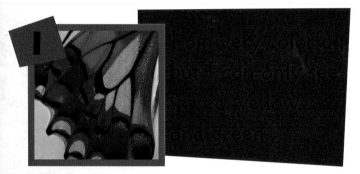 I am very colorful, but I can only see in red, yellow, and green.

4 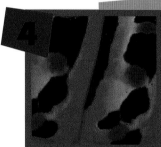 I eat and eat! I look like my food, so I am hard to spot.

2  My long legs look like leaves. If I stay still, you won't see me!

5 As I fly from flower to flower, my hairy legs are coated in pollen.

3 I have eight legs and I like jumping on my dinner!

6  Watch out! I have big pincers and a fierce sting.

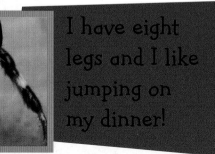

Answers: 1 Butterfly, 2 Stick insect, 3 Jumping spider, 4 Caterpillar, 5 Bee, 6 Scorpion.